The
North Wind
and
the Sun

For
AURELIE

© Brian Wildsmith 1964

First published 1964 by Oxford University Press

First American Publication 1964 by Franklin Watts, Inc.
575 Lexington Avenue, New York, N.Y. 10022
Second Impression 1964, Third Impression 1965,
Fourth Impression 1966, Fifth Impression 1968

Library of Congress Catalog Card Number: 64-13872

PRINTED IN AUSTRIA

A Fable by La Fontaine

THE
NORTH WIND
AND
THE SUN

Illustrated by

BRIAN WILDSMITH

FRANKLIN WATTS INCORPORATED
575 Lexington Avenue, New York, N.Y. 10022

One morning the North Wind and the Sun

saw a horseman
wearing a new cloak.

"That young man looks
very pleased with his
new cloak," said the
North Wind.
"But I could easily
blow it off his back
if I wanted to."
"I don't think you could,"
said the Sun.
"But let us both try
to do it. You can try first."

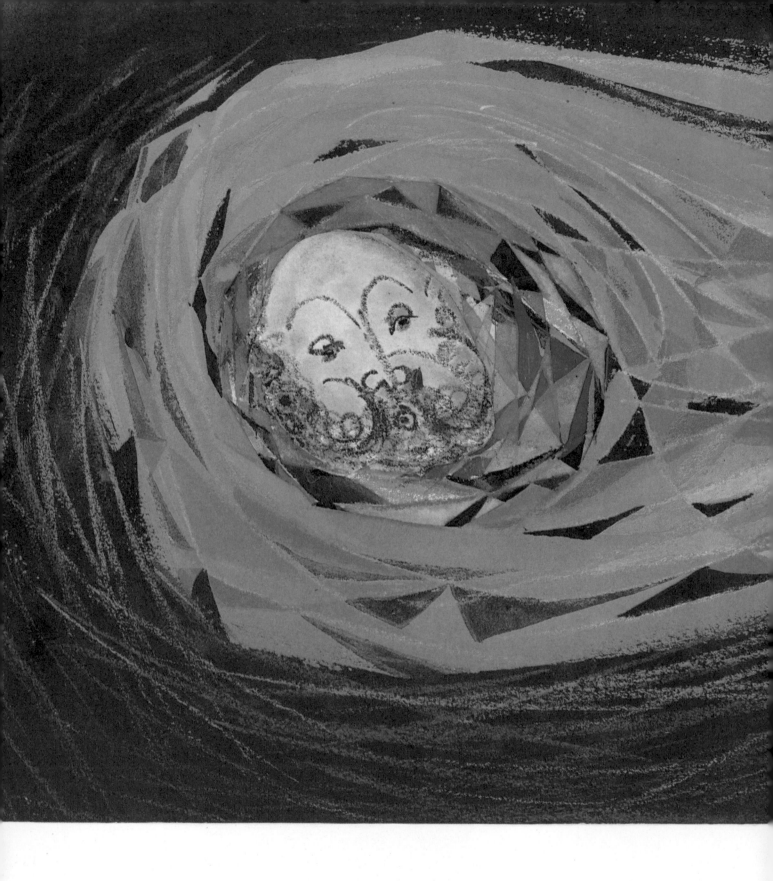

The North Wind began to

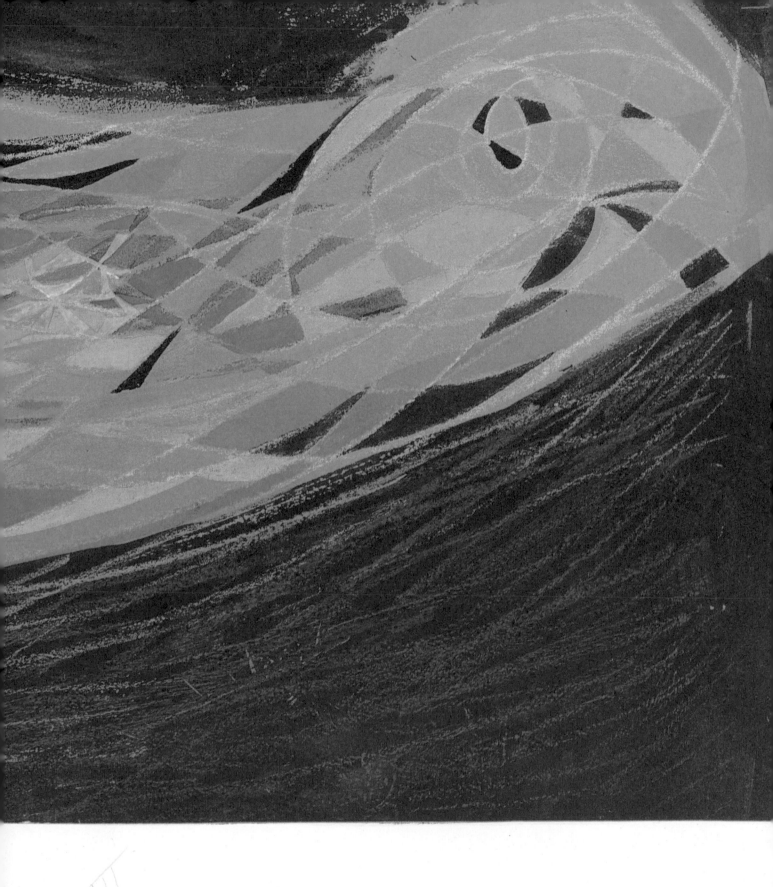

blow and blow and blow.

People
had to
chase after
their hats.

Leaves were blown from the trees.

All the animals were frightened.

The ships in the harbour were sunk.

The North Wind
blew with all
his might,
but it was no use,
for the horseman
just pulled
his cloak
more tightly
around him.

"My turn now,"
cried the Sun.

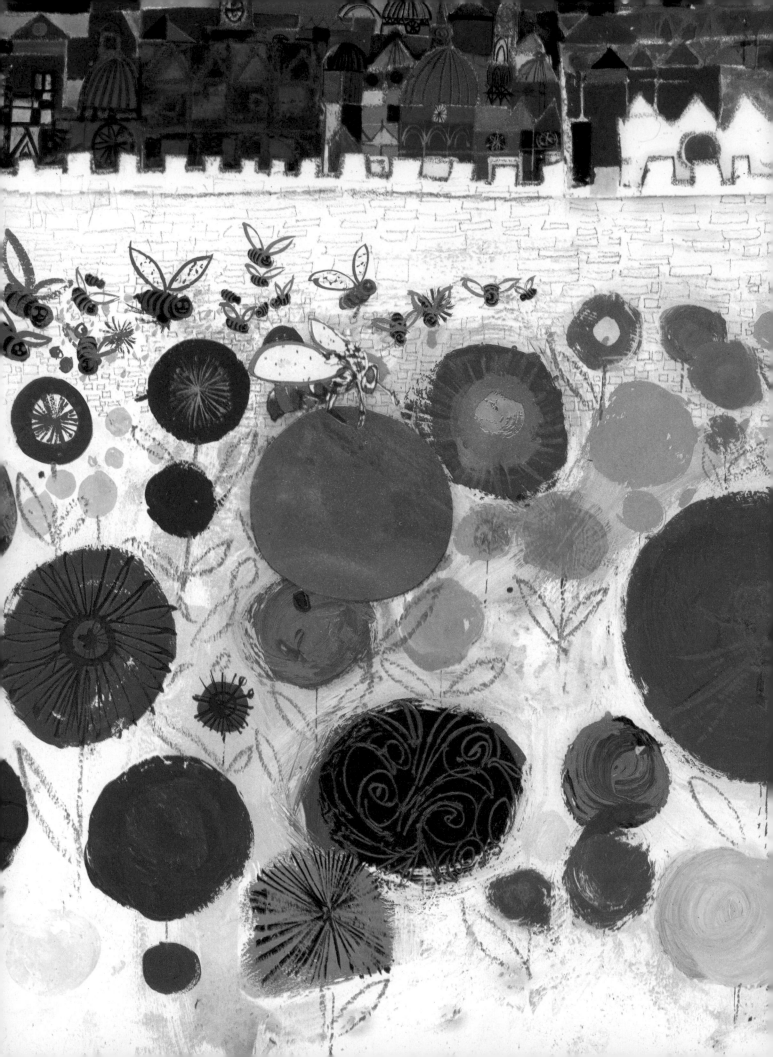

And as he gave out his gentle heat, insects hummed and flowers opened.

The birds began to sing.

The animals lay down to sleep.

And the people came out to gossip.

The horseman began to
feel very hot, and when he
came to a river
he took off his clothes
and went in for a swim.

So the Sun was able to achieve by warmth and gentleness what the North Wind in all his strength and fury could not do.